Big Trouble at Camp Little Big Top

"BEEP! BEEP! BEEEEEP!" A boy wearing clown makeup, baggy pants, and a bright orange wig rode into the circus ring on a tricycle. He was Orson Wong from Nancy's third-grade class.

"Woof!" Celeste the Hopscotch Poodle barked. Everyone laughed as she chased Orson's tricycle.

"Get her away from meeee!" Orson let out a gigantic sneeze. His red rubber nose flew right off his face!

"How can you be in the Chuckle Brigade if you keep sneezing your nose off?" asked Gunther, the camp's director.

"I have to be a clown!" Orson cried. He waved his gigantic shoe in the air. "I'm Bosco Bigfoot. And no one makes balloon animals like great Bosco Bigfoot!"

"Then what should we do, Orson?" Hilda, the other director of the circus camp, asked.

Orson shrugged. "Maybe you can get rid of Celeste?"

"Get rid of Celeste?" Hilda gasped. "Celeste is the star of the show!"

The Nancy Drew Notebooks

Available from MINSTREL Books

THE
NANCY DREW
NOTEBOOKS®

#42

Circus Act

CAROLYN KEENE
ILLUSTRATED BY JAN NAIMO JONES

A
MINSTREL®
BOOK

Published by POCKET BOOKS
New York London Toronto Sydney Singapore

A MINSTREL PAPERBACK *Original*

 A Minstrel Book published by
POCKET BOOKS, a division of Simon & Schuster, Inc.
1230 Avenue of the Americas, New York, NY 10020

ISBN: 0-7434-0690-7

First Minstrel Books printing May 2001

10 9 8 7 6 5 4 3 2 1

Cover art by Joanie Schwarz

Printed in the U.S.A.

PHX/✶

Circus Act

1

"Hurry! Hurry! Hurry!"

How do you know if there's an elephant in your refrigerator?" Nancy Drew's best friend George Fayne asked.

Eight-year-old Nancy tried to imagine an elephant stuffed in her refrigerator. "I don't know," she asked. "How?"

"His footprints are in the peanut butter!" George laughed.

Nancy's other best friend, Bess Marvin, wrinkled her nose. "Yuck!" she cried.

Nancy smiled. Ever since they had started circus camp a week ago George had come up with lots of elephant jokes.

The three best friends had gone to camp before but nothing like Camp Little Big Top. Each morning for two weeks the girls would meet in a real circus tent inside the park. After a half hour of warm-up exercises the twelve campers learned everything from stilt-walking and unicycling to making balloon animals.

The camp had real animals, too—like Celeste the Hopscotch Poodle and Splatter the baby elephant, who painted pictures with his trunk.

The camp felt like a real circus to Nancy—especially when the cotton candy cart came around at the end of each day.

George—whose real name was Georgia—tugged at the tights under her shimmery gold outfit. "Why do we have to wear our costumes today?" she asked.

"Because it's Monday and we're rehearsing for the Super Show," Bess reminded her cousin. She adjusted the feathery headdress over her long blond hair. "It's only five days away."

Nancy couldn't wait. On Saturday night the campers would demonstrate their circus skills in a show with costumes and music. Nancy had been picked to perform with Celeste the Hopscotch Poodle.

The girls sat down on a row of bleachers inside the tent. They had done their warm-up stretches. Now they were waiting to rehearse inside the circus ring.

"Why can't I do something great in the Super Show?" Bess asked.

"You are, Bess," Nancy said. "You're helping Splatter paint with his trunk."

"Everyone will be clapping for Splatter, not for me," Bess complained. "I'd rather do acrobatics like George is doing. Or swing on the trapeze."

George's dark curls bounced as she shook her head. "Bess, you're afraid of heights. And you can't do one cartwheel."

"Yes, I can," Bess argued. "I just hate messing up my hair!"

Nancy giggled. For cousins, Bess and George were in no way alike.

"Hi, guys!" a voice said.

Nancy turned around. She saw eight-year-old Amy Wilder sitting behind them. Amy had brown hair and eyes. Her family had just moved into the big yellow house across the street from the park.

"Hi, Amy," George said. "How can you tell if an elephant is in your refrigerator?"

"Hmm," Amy thought out loud. "If his footprints are in the ice cream?"

"Peanut butter, ice cream," Bess said. "Those elephants sure get around!"

Nancy noticed Amy's black top hat, bright red jacket, and tights. She looked like a real circus ringmaster.

"You're lucky to be the ringmaster in the Super Show, Amy," Bess said. "You get to introduce all the acts."

"Ladies and gentlemen and children of all ages!" George imitated Amy.

"Thanks, but I'd rather work with Celeste," Amy admitted. "I love dogs."

"Do you have a dog, Amy?" Nancy asked.

Amy shook her head. "But our new house is perfect for a dog," she said. "It has a huge yard, a porch, a clubhouse—"

"A clubhouse?" Bess shrieked. "You have your own clubhouse?"

"It's really a guest house," Amy admitted. "But it's a clubhouse to me."

"Neat!" Nancy said.

"I know!" Amy said excitedly. "Why don't you all come over to see it today?"

Nancy wanted to say yes, but she and Bess and George had other plans. Their friend Katie Zaleski had invited them to her house after camp.

Katie was videotaping her own TV show in her basement all summer. That afternoon she was interviewing Nancy about being the best detective in school.

"Sorry, Amy," Nancy said. "But we already made plans."

"Maybe another day," Amy said.

The girls turned back to the ring. Three kids had begun to swing across the tent on trapezes.

"Up, up, and awaaaaaay!" nine-year-old Joey Riccio shouted as he swung.

There was a net below him, and he wore a harness around his waist. Two other nine-year-olds, Lori Lasko and Tyrone Porter, stood on a platform, waiting their turn.

"The Great Flying Tremendoes are stupendo!" Lori shouted from the top.

Nancy rolled her eyes. Joey, Lori, and Tyrone liked to call themselves the Great Flying Tremendoes. Probably because they thought they were hot stuff!

The Flying Tremendoes climbed down the ladder. They each took a deep bow.

"I do that stuff in the playground every day," George whispered.

A man and woman dressed in gold leotards and white capes walked into the ring. They were Gunther and Hilda Weber, the directors of the circus camp.

The Webers had once been real circus performers in Europe. Now they traveled all over the United States with Camp Little Big Top. They taught all of the circus stunts and cared for the animals.

"Great, kids!" Gunther called after the Flying Tremendoes. "Just remember to keep your arms straight when you swing."

"The next act to rehearse will be Nancy and Celeste," Hilda announced.

Nancy straightened the headband in her reddish blond hair and jumped up from the bleachers.

Hilda led Celeste into the ring with one

hand. Her other hand held a blue hula hoop and a basket of blocks.

Nancy smiled when she saw Celeste. Her soft white fur was clipped in a fancy poodle style. Hilda even used a gentle pink hair dye on her head and tail.

Nancy loved Celeste so much that the Webers gave her special permission to feed Celeste at the end of camp each day.

"Hi, girl," Nancy said as she walked over to the dog. "We're a team, right?"

"BEEP! BEEP! BEEEEEP!"

Nancy jumped. A boy wearing clown makeup, baggy pants, and a bright orange wig rode into the ring on a tricycle. He was Orson Wong from Nancy's third-grade class.

"Woof!" Celeste barked. Everyone laughed as she chased Orson's tricycle.

"Get her away from meeee!" Orson yelled. He stopped his tricycle and let out a gigantic sneeze. His red rubber nose flew right off his face!

Orson ran to pick up his nose. "I thought I was next," he complained. "And that dog always makes me sneeze!"

"How can you be in the Chuckle Brigade if you keep sneezing your nose off?" Gunther asked.

"I have to be a clown!" Orson cried. He waved his giant shoe in the air. "I'm Bosco Bigfoot. And no one makes balloon animals like the great Bosco Bigfoot!"

"Then what should we do, Orson?" Hilda asked.

Orson shrugged. "Maybe you can get rid of Celeste?" he asked.

"Get rid of Celeste?" Hilda gasped. "Celeste is the star of the show!"

"The only poodle who uses her noodle," Gunther agreed.

"Okay, okay." Orson sighed. "It was just a suggestion."

Orson rode his tricycle to the bleachers. Nancy turned to the Webers. "May I start now?" she asked.

"Yes," Gunther said. He turned to the bleachers. "Amy, you're on!"

Amy walked into the ring and shouted as loud as she could: "Camp Little Big Top is proud to present—Nancy Drew and Celeste the Hopscotch Poodle!"

Nancy bowed. She picked up the blue hula hoop and turned to Celeste.

"Jump, Celeste!" she commanded.

Celeste stepped back. Then she leaped right through the hula hoop.

Nancy glanced at the bleachers. Bess and George were clapping. Orson was busily twisting another balloon animal.

It was time for Celeste's big trick. Nancy quickly placed the silver blocks on the ground one by one. When they were all in place, Nancy turned to Celeste.

"Hopscotch!" Nancy called.

Celeste stood up on her hind legs. She hopped over the blocks one by one.

Suddenly Nancy heard a loud pop.

Celeste stumbled. Then the white poodle began running out of the ring.

"Celeste!" Nancy cried. "Come back!"

2
Dog—Gone!

"**G**otcha!" Gunther said. He gently grabbed Celeste.

Nancy knew what the loud pop was. It was the sound of a balloon bursting. And she thought she knew who had burst it. She looked straight at Orson.

"It wasn't me!" Orson protested. "Joey grabbed my balloon and popped it."

"I didn't think it would scare anyone," Joey said with a shrug.

"You scared poor Celeste when you broke her concentration," Gunther scolded.

"Poor *Celeste?*" Orson complained. "What about my poor balloon giraffe?"

After Joey apologized, Celeste performed her hopscotch trick one more time. When Nancy's practice was over she handed Celeste to Hilda. Then Nancy walked out of the ring to the watercooler for a drink.

While Nancy sipped, she could see the Flying Tremendoes from the corner of her eye. They were wearing their silver capes and standing around the cotton candy cart.

"Why does that dog have to be in the show, anyway?" Tyrone was saying.

"We're the stars of the Super Show, not her!" Lori said angrily.

Nancy had a feeling that Joey had scared Celeste on purpose. She also had another feeling—she thought she saw Joey take a bag of cotton candy from the cart and stuff it under his cape!

Those three are bad news, Nancy thought as she walked to the bleachers.

Nancy forgot all about the Flying Tremendoes as she watched her friends practice. George did somersaults on the trampoline. Bess posed for Splatter as he painted her portrait with his trunk.

When the rehearsal was over the campers changed into their regular clothes and ate lunch in the park.

"Why do elephants wear sneakers?" George asked as she opened a milk carton.

"Why?" Amy asked.

"So they can sneak up on mice!" George said with a giggle.

"I don't get it," Bess said.

Nancy looked at her watch. "Time to feed Celeste!" she said happily.

Nancy had permission to go inside the tent. She walked to the back, where Splatter's pen and Celeste's big wire cage stood.

"Hi, Splatter! Hi, Celeste!" Nancy said. The baby elephant swung his trunk back and forth. Celeste wagged her tail.

Nancy turned to the bags of Dynamo Dog, Celeste's high-energy dog food.

There were always three bags of dog food: beef, chicken, and crunchy biscuits. Nancy was about to reach for the beef when she heard a thump-thump-thumping sound.

Nancy whirled around and saw Orson. He was still dressed in his Bosco Bigfoot costume—red nose and all.

"Hey." Orson held out a colorful can. "Want some peanut brittle?"

"No, thank you," Nancy said. She loved peanut brittle, but she didn't trust Orson.

"Aw, come on," Orson urged. "My mom made it. She'll be upset when she hears you didn't want it."

Nancy bit her lip. She liked Mrs. Wong and didn't want to upset her.

"Okay," Nancy said. She grabbed the can and twisted the lid. A long paper snake popped out, and Nancy shrieked.

Orson laughed but Nancy was mad.

"Why don't you save your tricks for the show?" Nancy snapped.

Celeste stuck her nose through the cage and growled at Orson.

"What's *her* problem?" Orson asked. Then he threw back his head and began to sneeze. "Ah, ah, ah—choooo!"

Orson's red nose flew off again. But this time it landed in Nancy's hands.

"Ewww!" Nancy said, dropping the nose on the ground. "Gross!"

"That dog is spoiling everything," Orson said. He scooped up his snake and stuffed it back in the can. "Everything!"

Orson stomped away. He forgot to pick up his rubber nose.

"Back to work." Nancy sighed. She filled Celeste's dish with beef dog food and slid it into her cage. Then she closed the cage door and brought down the latch.

Nancy tugged at the latch to make sure it was properly closed. It was.

"Nancy!" Bess called from outside the tent. "Gunther is giving out cherry vanilla cotton candy!"

"Coming!" Nancy called back. She wiggled her finger through the cage and smiled. "See you tomorrow, Celeste."

"Good day, River Heights!" Katie announced. "This is Katie Zaleski and Lester coming to you from my basement."

"Awwk!" Katie's parrot Lester squawked. "Good day! Good day!"

It was three o'clock in the afternoon. Nancy, Bess, and George were about to watch the videotaping of *The Katie and Lester Show.* Katie sat on a sofa with Lester on her shoulder. Her cousin Scooter pointed a video camera at them.

"My guest today is Nancy Drew," Katie said. "She's the best detective at Carl Sandburg Elementary School!"

"Yay, Nancy!" Bess and George cheered as Nancy joined Katie on the sofa.

"So, Nancy," Katie said with a grin. "What's it like being a detective?"

"Well, I have a blue detective notebook," Nancy said. "That's where I write down all my suspects and clues—"

"That's cool," Katie interrupted. "But let's talk about Celeste the Hopscotch Poodle. What is she like? Is she really pink and white? Do tell!"

Nancy was puzzled. She thought she was going to talk about being a detective.

"Celeste jumps through hula hoops," Nancy said. "And she hops over blocks."

"Awesome!" Katie cried. "And you're going to bring Celeste on my show, right?"

Nancy saw Scooter hold up a sign that read, YES! But she knew the answer was NO!

"No, Katie," Nancy said, shaking her head. "I can't take Celeste out of camp."

Katie stared at Nancy. Then she turned to the camera. "My next guest is Shirley, the school crossing guard. We'll find out what school crossing guards do when there's no school."

"Cut!" Scooter shouted. He shut off the video camera, and the girls stood up.

"We can't have a show without an animal act!" Scooter complained.

"I know some elephant jokes," George offered. "How do you know if an elephant—"

"Forget it," Katie snapped. "I have to call Shirley the school crossing guard. She's supposed to be here, and she's late."

As the girls left Katie's house Nancy felt bad. The last thing she wanted to do was disappoint a friend.

"You're hardly eating your barbecue chicken, Nancy," Mr. Drew said. He flipped a piece of chicken on the sizzling grill.

"Too much cotton candy?" Hannah joked. Hannah Gruen had been the Drews' housekeeper since Nancy was only three.

Nancy shook her head. She told her dad and Hannah all about Katie.

"I said I couldn't bring Celeste to her show," Nancy said. "Now I feel awful."

"You would have felt worse if you'd brought Celeste and got in trouble," Mr. Drew said. "It's better to tell the truth right away than feel bad later, right?"

"Right!" Nancy smiled. "You have the answer to everything, Daddy."

"He's not a bad cook, either!" Hannah said, taking a bite of chicken.

Nancy's puppy, Chocolate Chip, begged for scraps. But Nancy shook her head. "Even Celeste eats dog food," she told her.

After Nancy finished her dinner she went into the den and turned on the TV. Using the remote she looked for Katie's show on the River Heights Community Channel. Instead Nancy found a news flash.

"Mr. and Mrs. Weber," a reporter was saying. "Are you sure Celeste is missing?"

Nancy sat straight up in her chair.

"Celeste's cage door was left open," Hilda sobbed. "And now she's gone!"

Nancy froze.

"I didn't leave Celeste's cage open," Nancy thought out loud. "I didn't!"

3

Clowning Around

I hope Hilda and Gunther believe me," Nancy told Bess and George as they walked toward the circus tent the next morning.

"Don't worry, Nancy," Bess said. "No one will blame you. You'll see."

But as soon as the girls entered the circus tent . . .

"There she is!" a six-year-old camper cried. "She left Celeste's cage open!"

"But I *did* close the door," Nancy told the Webers. "And I latched it, too!"

"Not well enough," Gunther said.

Nancy's heart sank. She had told the truth. What more could she do?

George stepped up to the Webers. "Someone is bound to find Celeste sooner or later," she said. "They'll read her dog tag and know who she is. Right?"

"Wrong." Gunther sighed. "Celeste never wore a dog tag."

"But all dogs wear tags," Nancy said. She thought of Chocolate Chip and her heart-shaped tag.

"Celeste isn't just *any* dog," Gunther said. "She's a canine celebrity."

"Now we'll never get her back!" Hilda said, dabbing her eyes with her cape.

"Awesome!" Orson cheered. "I mean . . . that would be . . . awful."

Why is he so happy? Nancy wondered.

"Okay, kids," Gunther said. "Put on your costumes now. The clowns will rehearse with me first. All other campers will do warm-up exercises with Hilda."

"What about me?" Nancy asked in a small voice. "Should I put on my costume?"

Gunther heaved a big sigh. "You might

as well. In case Celeste comes back."

"Fat chance," Orson muttered.

"Orson," Gunther said, "you'll be tumbling today. So you can leave your big shoes in the costume room."

Orson looked disappointed. "What's Bosco Bigfoot without his big shoes?"

"A pest!" George mumbled.

All of the campers stared at Nancy as they headed toward the costume area.

"This isn't fair," Nancy told Bess and George. "Someone else left the cage open. Either on purpose or by mistake."

"How can you prove it?" George asked.

"With this!" Nancy pulled her blue notebook out of her pocket.

Nancy carried her detective notebook everywhere. But she hadn't thought she'd need it at circus camp.

Opening the notebook to a fresh page, Nancy wrote, "Where is Celeste?"

"Someone could have stolen Celeste," Nancy thought out loud. "But who?"

"I bet Splatter knows," Bess said. "His pen is right next to Celeste's cage."

"Elephants never forget, but they don't talk either," Nancy said. "Let's search Celeste's cage for clues."

"But what about our warm-up exercises?" George asked.

Nancy looked at her watch. "They won't start for another fifteen minutes. We still have some time."

Gunther and Hilda were busy setting up the ring. Nancy, Bess, and George hurried over to Celeste's empty cage.

The first thing Nancy did was search the dirt ground for footprints. She saw something that made her eyes fly open.

"Look!" Nancy said, pointing down. "A trail of *paw* prints!"

Nancy studied the prints. They led from the cage to an opening in the tent.

"If Celeste made those prints," Bess said, "it shows that she walked out."

"And she wasn't alone," Nancy said. She placed her own sneakered foot inside a giant footprint. "There's also a trail of huge footprints next to the paw prints."

"You mean someone with big feet led Celeste out of the tent?" George asked.

"Big feet?" Bess asked. She narrowed her eyes. "As in Bosco Bigfoot?"

"Orson said Celeste made him sneeze," Nancy pointed out. "He also seemed pretty glad when Celeste disappeared."

Nancy had her first suspect. She wrote the word "suspects," then Orson's name right below it.

"Some other clowns have big shoes, too," Nancy said. "We really should match Orson's shoe with the print to be sure."

Bess squeezed her nose. "You mean touch Orson's shoe?"

"It's a stinky job, but somebody's got to do it," Nancy said. "As soon as the clowns are in the ring we'll go into the costume room. Then we'll grab Orson's shoe and compare it to the footprint."

"Gotcha," George said.

The girls waited until all the clowns were in the ring. Then they raced to the costume room. It was behind a white canvas curtain painted with colorful animals.

Nancy peeked behind the curtain. "No other campers," she said in a low voice. "The coast is clear."

The girls slipped into the costume room. The hooks and racks were filled with costumes. A cubby shelf stood against the side of the tent. Two more curtains served as dressing areas.

"Check it out," George said. She grabbed a big rubber horn and tooted it.

"Shh!" Nancy warned. She found Orson's cubby right away. It was the one with the fake peanut brittle can inside.

Nancy pulled a big shoe out of the cubby. She slipped it under her arm.

"All systems go," Nancy said. She was about to turn when George grabbed her arm.

"Listen!" George hissed.

Nancy did listen. She heard a strange putt-putt-putt sound. Someone was coming. Or something!

"Quick!" Nancy said. "Let's hide!"

George pointed the rubber horn toward a costume rack. "Behind there!"

Putt-putt-putt-putt!

The girls ran behind velvet jackets and ruffled dresses.

Nancy held her breath as they peeked

out. A tiny yellow car was rolling around the curtain and into the costume room!

Putt-putt-putt-putt!

The car stopped. A door opened and Orson Wong stepped out. Then another clown. And another. And another. Until the whole Chuckle Brigade had filed out!

Nancy stared at the clowns. They each had a rubber nose and a plastic daisy on their jackets.

Orson walked over to his cubby. He pulled out one shoe. But when he reached for the other one he began to shout: "My shoe is missing! Nobody leave the tent!"

Orson's loud voice startled Nancy. She stumbled back—right against George's rubber horn!

"BEEEEEP! BEEEEEEP!"

Nancy froze. She could practically feel the clowns staring right at the rack.

Oh, great, Nancy thought.

Busted!

4
Working for Peanuts

T here's your shoe, Orson," a small clown with a green wig said as the girls stepped out.

"Ah-ha!" Orson pointed to his shoe under Nancy's arm. "Everyone wants to walk in the shoes of the great Bosco Bigfoot."

"In your dreams!" George sneered.

The clowns lined up shoulder to shoulder.

"Okay, gang," Orson told the other clowns. "Ready, aim—*spray!*"

The girls shrieked. The daisies on the clowns' jackets were squirting water!

Nancy dropped Orson's shoe as she tried to cover her face.

When the daisies dripped their last drops, a sputtering Nancy turned to Orson.

"That was sneaky!" Nancy scolded.

"We were just clowning around," the green-wigged clown said with a grin.

"You were supposed to laugh," another clown wearing droopy overalls said.

But Nancy, Bess, and George were not laughing.

"What were you doing near Celeste's cage?" Nancy demanded. "We saw your big footprints next to her paw prints!"

For a moment Orson thought about that. Then he shrugged. "Yesterday after cotton candy I went back for my nose. The one I sneezed off, remember?" he asked.

"I remember." Nancy shuddered when she thought of the wet nose in her hand.

"After I picked it up I walked out of the tent," Orson explained. *"Alone."*

"Was Celeste still in her cage?" Nancy asked.

"Yeah," Orson said. "Growling at me as usual."

Nancy stared at Orson. "Is that the whole truth?" she asked.

"You bet!" Orson said. He held out his hand. "Let's shake on it."

"Don't do it, Nancy!" George warned.

But Nancy had never turned down a handshake. It wouldn't be polite.

Nancy sighed. She grabbed Orson's hand and jumped. He had a small tickly buzzer tucked in his palm.

Orson rocked back and forth as he laughed—until he began to sneeze.

"Ahhh-choooo! Ahhh-choooo!"

The girls ducked as Orson's nose flew over their heads.

"You see that?" Orson complained. "Celeste may be gone, but her fur is everywhere."

Orson put on his nose and his big shoes. Then he turned to the other clowns. "Come on, you guys. Let's practice tossing those cream pies."

Nancy watched as the clowns marched out of the costume room.

"Orson is no longer a suspect," she said. "But he'll always be a pest."

After Nancy crossed Orson's name out of her notebook the girls changed into their own costumes. Then they joined Hilda and the others for warm-up exercises.

"By the way, Nancy," Hilda said. "If Celeste isn't found by tomorrow you'll have to do something else in the show."

Nancy's heart sank. She didn't want to do anything else. She wanted to work with Celeste.

I'm going to find Celeste, Nancy thought, if it's the last thing I do!

While everyone practiced their circus acts Nancy kept busy juggling beanbags. During the juice break, she, Bess, and George returned to the scene of the crime.

Nancy walked around Celeste's cage. She stopped next to the pile of dog food.

"That's weird," Nancy said. "I fed Celeste beef dog food yesterday. Now the whole bag of beef is gone."

"So?" George asked.

"So whoever took Celeste might be feeding her, too," Nancy decided.

"You mean someone may be *hiding*

Celeste?" Bess asked. "Who would do that?"

Nancy wasn't sure—until she saw the Flying Tremendoes walking through the tent on their hands.

"Show-offs," Bess said. "They still think they're the stars."

"Exactly!" Nancy cried. "The Flying Tremendoes could be hiding Celeste until the show is over. That way they can be the stars of the Super Show!"

Nancy added the Flying Tremendoes to her suspect list. She was about to shut her notebook when a splash of bright blue paint landed on her page.

"Hey!" Nancy complained. She glanced up and saw Splatter the elephant. He was in his pen, painting on white paper.

The girls moved closer to get a better look. The painting looked like a dog made out of sticks.

"That's the funniest-looking dog I ever saw," Bess said.

"He's an elephant," George argued. "What do you expect—the *Mona Lisa?*"

"I wonder if Splatter is painting Celeste," Nancy said slowly. "If he saw who took Celeste, he might be trying to tell us something with his painting."

"How would we know?" George asked.

"I'm going to have Splatter do a composite sketch," Nancy announced.

"A what?" Bess asked.

"My dad took me to visit a police station once," Nancy said. "A woman was telling an artist how to draw the thief who stole her purse."

"So Splatter can paint the thief who stole Celeste," George said, her eyes flashing. "I like it. I like it."

Nancy placed a clean sheet of paper on the floor of Splatter's pen.

"Splatter?" Nancy asked. "Who opened the cage yesterday and took Celeste?"

Splatter swung his trunk back and forth. Then he dipped his paintbrush into the pots of paint and began to paint.

"Go, Splatter!" the girls cheered as the elephant slopped paint on the paper.

When Splatter was done he tossed the painting out of his pen. It was a picture of a girl with shoulder-length brown hair.

"Look familiar?" George asked.

"Not yet," Nancy said. "There are lots of girls at camp with medium-length brown hair."

"But only one elephant who can paint," Bess said proudly. "I'm glad I'm working with Splatter!"

Nancy waved the painting dry. Then she slipped it into her notebook. Maybe it would make sense later.

The girls spent the rest of the morning learning how to march in the Super Show parade. Amy led the parade and carried a big banner with the camp name.

I hope Amy still invites us to her clubhouse, Nancy thought. But more than anything I hope I find Celeste.

After camp the girls ran to Nancy's house to watch *The Katie and Lester Show*. But when they turned on the TV, the show had already started.

"Oh, rats!" George said. "We must have missed your part, Nancy."

"Shirley the school crossing guard has something called bunions," Katie was saying. "So my guest today is Brandon. He sells ice cream at the River Heights swimming pool."

"Hey," Brandon said nervously.

"Brandon," Katie said. "Of all your years selling ice cream, which flavor melts faster? Chocolate or vanilla?"

Lester stretched his feathery neck toward Brandon. Then he yanked Brandon's glasses off with his beak.

"Hey!" Brandon cried. "Tell cracker-breath to quit it!"

"Uh-oh!" Lester squawked. "Arrrk!"

Nancy and her friends giggled.

"Okay, okay," Katie said to the camera. "Our next show will be super-duper special. Our guest will be the most amazing, awesome dog in the world! And wait until you see what she does!"

"Ruff, ruff!" Lester squawked.

An amazing dog?

Nancy stared at Bess and George. There was only one amazing dog they knew.

"Bess, George!" Nancy cried. "Could Katie be talking about Celeste?"

5

Snoops and Hoops

Maybe Katie didn't say 'dog,'"Bess said. "Maybe she said . . . pig."

"Since when do pigs go 'ruff, ruff'?" George asked.

"Katie did want Celeste on her show more than anything," Nancy said. "And Katie does have shoulder-length brown hair, just like the girl in Splatter's painting."

"But Katie's our friend," George said.

"I know, I know," Nancy groaned. She couldn't imagine Katie going to the circus camp and taking Celeste. But a detective had to consider all possibilities.

"Are you going to write Katie's name in your notebook, Nancy?" Bess asked.

"I'll write it in *pencil*." Nancy sighed. "A pencil with a big, fat eraser."

Nancy wrote Katie's name in her notebook. Then she looked at her watch.

"Katie usually tapes her new show around now," Nancy said. "Let's go to her house and check out that amazing dog."

The girls walked the short distance to Katie's house. As they neared the Zaleskis' front yard Nancy noticed something strange. There was a stack of colorful hula hoops on the grass.

"Katie doesn't play with hula hoops," Bess said. "She says they make her dizzy."

"Unless," Nancy said slowly, "the hula hoops are for Celeste."

Bess let out a little gasp.

"If Celeste is here, she might be in Katie's basement," George said. "That's where she videotapes her show."

The girls raced across the yard to Katie's house. Nancy saw a small window at the bottom of the house. It was just inches up from the ground.

"I'll bet that's the basement window," Nancy whispered. "Let's see if we can see something down there."

The girls kneeled by the window. Nancy peeked inside. She couldn't see much, but she could hear a low howling noise. It sounded just like a dog.

"Katie *does* have a dog down there!" Nancy whispered.

"Is it pink and white?" Bess asked.

Nancy pressed her nose against the window. "I think I see—"

"Arrrk!"

Nancy gasped. Lester the parrot flew up against the window. He flapped his wings against the glass and screeched: "Peekaboo! Peekaboo! Arrrk!"

Bess shrieked as the girls fell back on the grass.

"Hey!" Nancy heard Scooter shout. "Someone is spying on our show!"

"Busted by a parrot," George groaned.

Katie and Scooter ran out of the house. They stood over the girls.

"Why were you peeking in my basement

window?" Katie asked. She looked more confused than angry.

"Peekaboo!" Lester squawked from Katie's shoulder. "Raaaak!"

Nancy dusted herself off and stood up. "We wanted to see the amazing dog you said you had," she said.

"No problem," Katie said. She put two fingers in her mouth and whistled loudly. After a few seconds a little gray dog ran out of the house.

"Meet Toby," Katie declared. "Toby the singing schnauzer."

Nancy stared at the dog. He was cute. But he was definitely not Celeste.

"He's *my* dog!" Scooter said proudly. "I taught him myself."

"No way," George said. "Dogs might be able to hopscotch, but they can't sing."

"That's what you think," Katie said. She turned to her cousin. "Hit it, Scoot!"

Scooter took a harmonica out of his pocket. Then he began to play.

"'She'll be comin' round the mountain when she comes,'" Katie sang.

"Yee-haaa!" Lester screeched.

Toby threw back his fuzzy head. Then he opened his mouth and began to howl.

Nancy and Bess giggled. But George clapped her hands over her ears.

"Put a sock in it!" George begged.

Toby stopped howling. He wagged his tail happily.

Nancy knew that Katie didn't have Celeste. But she still had one question.

"Katie?" she asked. "Why are all those hula hoops in your yard?"

"Oh, those are for Lydia," Katie said. She pointed over Nancy's shoulder. "The other act in the show."

Nancy spun around. A girl wearing a sparkly leotard was running into the yard.

"I'm ready for my close-up, you guys!" Lydia said with a giggle.

Lydia picked up three hula hoops. She twirled them on her arms and one leg.

"She giggles a lot," Scooter said. "But she's better than ice-cream boy."

Nancy smiled. All the pieces had fallen into place, and Katie hadn't taken Celeste.

Lydia was spinning three hoops around

her neck when Nancy, Bess, and George left Katie's yard.

"That Toby was funny," Bess said.

"A real howl!" George joked.

Suddenly Nancy heard a rumbling noise. She looked up and saw Joey, Lori, and Tyrone speeding down the block on in-line skates.

"Beep! Beep!" Joey yelled. He and Tyrone were eating bags of blue cotton candy as they skated. Lori was holding a big white envelope under her arm.

"Slow down!" Nancy shouted.

The Flying Tremendoes swerved on their skates. Then they fell to the ground in a big heap. Joey and Tyrone dropped their bags of cotton candy. Bunches of papers flew out of Lori's white envelope.

"See what you made us do!" Tyrone complained.

"Some acrobats!" George said, shaking her head. "You can't even roller-skate!"

Nancy read one of the papers on the sidewalk: "Hurry, hurry, hurry! See the stars of the Super Show—the Great Flying Tremendoes!"

"What are these?" Nancy demanded.

"We made those flyers ourselves," Joey bragged. "Now everyone will know who the *real* stars of the show are."

"But Celeste is the star and you know it," Nancy argued.

"Not anymore," Tyrone said. "Celeste is history. The Flying Tremendoes rule!"

Lori, Joey, and Tyrone gave one another high fives. They picked up the flyers and skated away.

"You forgot your cotton candy!" Bess called. She waved the two bags in the air.

"They forgot this, too," Nancy said. She picked up a yellow piece of paper from the sidewalk and studied it.

"What is it, Nancy?" George asked.

"It's the order slip from the copy shop," Nancy said. "The Flying Tremendoes had those flyers made up last week. *Before* Celeste was missing."

"What does that mean?" Bess asked.

Nancy narrowed her eyes.

"It means the Flying Tremendoes might have known that Celeste would be gone!"

6

Food for Thought

Maybe the Flying Tremendoes *are* hiding Celeste!" Bess gasped. "So they can be the stars of the show!"

Nancy opened her notebook to her clue list. She wrote the words "order slip." Then she wrote the date of the order and the date that Celeste disappeared.

"What an awesome clue!" George said.

"I have another clue," Bess said. "Why were the Flying Tremendoes eating blue cotton candy when the cotton candy we ate in camp today was yellow and white?"

"Bess!" George said, rolling her eyes.

"What does cotton candy have to do with a missing poodle?"

"I don't know." Bess tucked the cotton candy under her arm. "Just food for thought."

Nancy shut her detective notebook. "We'll question the Flying Tremendoes first thing tomorrow morning," she said.

"What if they don't tell the truth?" Bess asked.

"Then the Flying Tremendoes," Nancy said, "will be the *Lying* Tremendoes!"

That night Nancy lay in bed but couldn't sleep. She turned on her night-light and opened her notebook. Then she unfolded Splatter's painting and spread it across her bed.

If the Flying Tremendoes took Celeste, Nancy wondered, then why did Splatter just paint one girl?

Nancy noticed something clsc. The girl in the painting was wearing purple sneakers. Who at camp had purple sneakers?

Nancy turned off her night-light and snuggled under her quilt.

Purple sneakers, cotton candy, painting elephants! Nancy thought as she drifted off to sleep. This case is turning into a three-ring circus!

"What do you call a flying elephant?" George asked the next morning in the circus tent.

"What?" Nancy asked.

"A jumbo jet!" George laughed.

"I hope he remembers to pack his trunk," Bess added. "Get it? Get it?"

"I get it," Nancy said. But she wasn't really laughing. She was too busy checking out the campers' feet.

No purple sneakers, Nancy thought. Just acrobat slippers and clown shoes.

Nancy saw Joey, Lori, and Tyrone inside the ring. They were standing on their heads with their backs to the girls.

"Ew!" Bess said. "They're going to get sawdust in their hair."

Nancy pressed one finger to her lips. She waved her friends closer to the ring.

"Good job, you guys!" Nancy heard Lori say. "No one will ever find it now."

"Yeah," Joey sneered. "We hid it nice and good!"

Nancy stared at Bess and George. What did they hide? Celeste?

"Oh, Nancy!" a voice called out.

Nancy spun around. Hilda and Gunther were walking toward them.

"Celeste has not been found yet," Hilda said. "So we've decided to make you a member of the Chuckle Brigade."

"You mean a clown?" Nancy gulped when she imagined herself with a weird wig and a red rubber nose. "What do I have to do?"

"It's easy," Gunther said. "All you have to do is stand still while Bosco Bigfoot throws a pie in your face."

"Bosco Bigfoot?" Nancy cried.

She saw Orson holding a cream pie and smiling slyly. "I hope you like lemon meringue," he snickered.

Nancy felt sick. It was bad enough that Celeste was missing. Now she had to get a pie in her face, too!

"Go to the costume room and pick out a clown costume," Hilda told Nancy. "Then you can practice with the other clowns."

"Don't worry, Nancy," Bess said as the Webers walked away. "We'll help you pick out a real funny costume."

"And if that's not funny enough," George said, "try an elephant joke."

Nancy knew her best friends were trying to make her feel better.

"Thanks, but I'm *not* going to be a clown in the Super Show," Nancy said. "I'm going to investigate the Flying Tremendoes, and then I'm going to find Celeste!"

The girls did not go straight to the costume room. They stopped off at the animal tent to look for more clues.

"Look!" Nancy said. "Now the bag of dog biscuits is missing."

"You don't think Splatter is eating the dog food, do you?" Bess asked.

"Not unless it has peanuts," George said.

Nancy heard footsteps outside the tent. She waved her friends to the opening and looked outside. Her eyes opened wide.

The Flying Tremendoes were running away from the tent and into the park. They were clutching their capes around them.

"Why are they wearing their capes?" George said. "They weren't before."

"Unless they're hiding something underneath those capes," Nancy said. "Like the bags of dog food."

"Nancy!" Bess exclaimed. "They might be bringing the dog food to Celeste!"

"Let's follow them!" Nancy said.

But when the girls ran into the park, they couldn't find the Flying Tremendoes.

The girls knew not to walk too far into the park. They stopped under a tree and looked around.

"Where did they go?" George asked.

"Who knows?" Bess said. She pointed at the ground. "But don't step in that yucky pink and white stuff."

"What pink and white stuff?" Nancy asked. She looked on the ground and saw four strands of pink and white fluff.

"It looks like pink and white fur!" Nancy exclaimed. "Celeste must be around here somewhere!"

7

Hide and Sneak!

Here's another piece!" George said. She picked up a strand of white fluff.

"And another!" Bess pointed to some fluff stuck to the trunk of the tree.

"I don't get it," Nancy said. "If Celeste's fur is here, then where is Cel—"

Nancy didn't finish her sentence. Clumps of pink and white fur were suddenly falling down from the tree.

"Hey!" George shouted.

"It's raining poodle fur!" Bess cried as a clump of fluff fell on her head.

Nancy looked up. She saw the Flying

Tremendoes sitting up in the tree and eating cherry vanilla cotton candy.

"Looking for something?" Tyrone asked. He was lying back on one of the tree branches and grinning.

Nancy felt a bit silly. The pink and white poodle fur was really cotton candy.

"We're looking for Celeste the Hopscotch Poodle!" Nancy yelled up.

"You said you were hiding something," George said. "We heard it ourselves!"

Joey, Lori, and Tyrone looked nervous— as if they really were hiding something.

"Come down from that tree!" Nancy demanded. "So we can talk about it."

"Okay." Joey popped a clump of cotton candy into his mouth. "But if you want to talk, you all have to come up here."

"But it's high," Bess complained.

"Du-uh!" Joey said. "No one climbs as high as the Flying Tremendoes!"

"Up, up, and awaaaay!" the Flying Tremendoes announced.

Bess put her hands on her hips and glared up at the tree.

"You think you're so great," Bess shouted.

"But you're not the best tree climbers in River Heights!"

"Then who is?" Tyrone demanded.

Bess pointed to George. "She is."

"I am?" George gasped. Then she grinned. "Yeah . . . I am!"

"Go for it, George!" Nancy cheered.

George marched to the tree, hugged the trunk, and inched her way up. Then she grabbed onto a branch with one hand.

The branch began to shake. Nancy jumped as a bag of blue cotton candy fell from the tree. Then another. And another.

Nancy ducked as more bags of colorful cotton candy fell down from the tree.

So that's it! Nancy thought. The Flying Tremendoes didn't steal Celeste. They stole cotton candy and hid it up in the tree!

"Ah-ha!" Bess cried. "I knew there was something fishy about that cotton candy yesterday."

"Good work, Bess," Nancy said. "You really did get some evidence."

"Yeah." Bess blushed. "Except I ate most of it."

"Okay, okay," Joey said as the Flying Tremendoes climbed down from the tree. "You caught us—sticky-handed."

"We thought you were hiding Celeste," Nancy said.

"Celeste?" Tyrone scoffed. "No way!"

"Then why did you have those flyers made up before Celeste was even missing?"

"The ones that said you were the stars of the Super Show," George added.

"Because we knew we were the real stars," Lori bragged. "Whether that dog was here or not."

Tyrone looked worried. "You're not going to tell Gunther and Hilda about the cotton candy, are you?" he asked.

"You can't!" Joey begged. "If they find out, the Flying Tremendoes will be up, up, and out of here."

"What you did was wrong," Nancy said. "But we won't tell as long as you put that cotton candy back into the cart."

"Fine with me," Tyrone said. "I was planning to do that anyway."

"Because you were beginning to feel guilty?" Nancy asked hopefully.

"No!" Tyrone grabbed his middle. "Because I was beginning to feel *sick!*"

While the Flying Tremendoes gathered the cotton candy bags Nancy and her friends returned to the tent.

"That rules out the Great Flying Tremendoes," George said.

"And leaves me with zero suspects." Nancy sighed. She remembered the Chuckle Brigade. "And a pie in my face!"

With the help of Bess and George, Nancy picked out a clown costume. It had a rainbow wig, baggy polka-dotted pants, and a striped jacket.

Nancy spent the rest of the morning practicing with the clowns. She held one end of a jump rope while another clown jumped on stilts.

"And now for my big finish!" Orson announced. He lifted the pie in his hand and aimed it straight at Nancy.

Oh, noooo! Nancy squeezed her eyes shut. She expected to hear a splat but instead she heard a loud "Ah-ah-ah-ah-chooooooo!" Then a splat.

Nancy opened her eyes. Orson had

sneezed and jammed his own face into the lemon meringue pie!

Nancy giggled. Maybe being a clown wasn't so bad after all!

After the rehearsals, the kids ate lunch. When Gunther wheeled out the cotton candy cart he looked puzzled.

"This is very strange," Gunther said. "Yesterday the cart was half empty. Now it's completely full."

Nancy smiled. She may not have found Celeste, but she did find missing cotton candy. That was better than nothing.

"Bess, George," Nancy said. "Why don't you come to my house after camp? Hannah said she'd bake circus cookies."

"What about Celeste?" Bess asked. "You're not giving up, are you, Nancy?"

"No," Nancy said. "But even detectives need a milk and cookie break."

Just then Nancy saw Amy carrying a big duffel bag on her shoulder.

"That looks heavy," Nancy called to Amy.

"It's my costume," Amy said, quickly. "I'm taking it home to wash."

That's funny, Nancy thought. The Webers sent all of the costumes to a laundry service to be cleaned.

"We still want to see your clubhouse, Amy," George said. "It sounds awesome."

Amy's face grew pale. "My clubhouse? Can't! Not yet! It's too messy!"

Nancy watched as Amy hurried to the cotton candy cart.

"Who cares if it's messy?" George asked. "She should see my room."

Nancy didn't get it either. Suddenly Amy didn't want them to see her clubhouse.

The girls walked to the back of the cotton candy line. Nancy saw Amy reaching into the cart for a bag. Then she noticed something else.

Amy's sneakers were bright purple!

8

Doggy in the Window

Bess! George!" Nancy whispered. "I think I know who may have taken Celeste!"

"Who?" Bess whispered.

"Amy is wearing purple sneakers," Nancy said. "Plus, she's carrying a heavy bag, which might be holding the dog food."

"Hey!" George said. "Do you think Amy is hiding Celeste in her clubhouse?"

Nancy watched as Amy walked across the street to her house.

"I don't know," Nancy said. "But I think we should visit Amy after camp."

"What if Amy doesn't let us in her house?" Bess asked.

"She will," Nancy said, smiling. "When she sees Hannah's circus cookies!"

After camp the girls had milk and cookies at Nancy's house. Then they carried a plate of cookies to Amy's house.

"Amy is playing in the guest house," Mrs. Wilder said after she opened the door. "Why don't you surprise her with those yummy-looking cookies?"

The girls walked around the yellow house to the backyard. Nancy saw a much smaller house. It had green shutters and was surrounded by trees.

That's the clubhouse, Nancy thought.

The girls hurried over to the little house. Nancy knocked on the door.

"Amy?" Nancy called. "Are you there?"

No one answered.

The girls raced to a window. They stood on their toes and peeked through.

"This window is too high," Bess said. She jumped up and down on her toes.

"Yeah," George said. "Even if Celeste is in

there, we won't be able to see her. Not unless she hops up."

Nancy's eyes lit up. "Did you say hops up?" she cried. "That's it!"

Bess and George looked puzzled as Nancy stepped back. She cupped her hands around her mouth and began to shout: "Hopscotch! Hopscotch! Hopscotch!"

George shook her head. "Nancy, what are you—"

Suddenly a big white poodle with a pink tuft of hair began bouncing past the window on her hind legs!

"It's Celeste!" the girls cried at the same time.

Amy ran around the clubhouse. Her mouth fell open, and she dropped the big bag of dog food she was holding. Nancy could see that it was the Dynamo Dog Biscuits.

"W-w-what are you doing by my clubhouse?" Amy stammered.

"You mean, *doghouse*," Nancy said.

Amy stared down at her purple sneakers. "I didn't steal Celeste if that's what you're thinking," she said.

"Then why is she here?" Nancy asked.

Amy dragged her sneaker in the dirt. Then she took a deep breath.

"Monday afternoon I sneaked back to the tent to play with Celeste," Amy said. "I made sure the Webers didn't see me when I opened the cage."

"*You* left the cage door open?" Bess asked.

"I closed it but forgot to latch it," Amy explained. "It was an accident!"

So that's who left the latch up, Nancy thought. Amy!

"Celeste followed me home," Amy went on. "I thought I'd play with her awhile in my clubhouse and then return her. I guess I played too long because when I went back to the park it was closed."

"You could have brought her back the next day," George said.

Amy shook her head. "Everyone knew how much I wanted a dog," she said. "I was afraid they'd think I'd *stolen* Celeste!"

Nancy felt a bit sorry for Amy. If she had told the truth in the beginning this would never have happened.

"We'll help you return Celeste," Nancy said. "If you promise to tell Gunther and Hilda the truth."

Amy thought about that. Then she smiled. "It's a deal!" she said.

The girls waited until Amy brought Celeste out of the clubhouse.

"Hi, Celeste," George said. "Long time no see."

Celeste wagged her tail as she followed the girls.

"Come on, girl," Nancy said gently. "You're going home."

"Beep! Beep!"

Nancy looked up. She saw Orson riding past Amy's house on a bicycle. He was wearing his Bosco Bigfoot costume.

"Not again!" Nancy groaned.

Celeste glared at Orson and growled. Then she barked, kicked up her heels, and began chasing Orson's bicycle.

"Celeste, stop!" Amy yelled. The four girls raced up the sidewalk after Celeste.

"Call her off!" Orson shouted as he rode his bike into the park.

"Woof!" Celeste barked.

The girls dashed into the park, too. Nancy watched as Orson fell off his bike, right in front of the circus tent.

"Get her off meeee!" Orson cried as Celeste began licking his red nose.

Gunther and Hilda ran out of the tent. They smiled when they saw Celeste.

"Where did you find her?" Hilda asked. She had happy tears in her eyes.

Amy stepped forward and told the Webers everything.

"I should have told you sooner," Amy said. "I'm really sorry."

"Apology accepted," Hilda said. She turned to Nancy. "And we're sorry for not believing you, Nancy."

"Apology accepted," Nancy said with a grin.

Gunther scratched Celeste around her neck. "From now on Celeste will wear a dog tag, like a normal dog."

"Perhaps a solid gold dog tag," Hilda added.

"Ahhh-choooo!" Orson sneezed and his nose went flying in the air.

"And as for you, Orson," Gunther said. "I think you should find out what's really making you sneeze."

"I did." Orson sniffed. "It's the red rubber nose. But I never told you because I didn't want to stop being a clown."

Nancy rolled her eyes. All this time Orson had been blaming Celeste!

"I suppose we can *paint* your nose red, Orson," Gunther said.

"You can do that?" Orson asked.

"Not me," Gunther said. "But Splatter the elephant is pretty good with a brush."

Nancy giggled. She could tell Gunther was joking, but Orson looked pretty worried.

Gunther and Hilda went into their trailer to call the news reporters.

"That was close!" Orson said. "I thought they'd boot me from circus camp."

"Don't worry, Orson," Nancy said with a smirk. "You'll *always* be a clown. As long as you live!"

"Really?" Orson said. His eyes lit up. "Thanks!"

Nancy watched as Orson hopped on his

bike and rode away. Celeste barked, but this time she didn't chase him.

"I'm going to miss having Celeste in my clubhouse," Amy said with a sigh.

"You can come to my house and play with Chocolate Chip anytime," Nancy said.

"Thanks, Nancy." Amy smiled. "I think I'm going to like River Heights!"

On Saturday night the circus show was a big success. Celeste performed her tricks like a star. With Bess's help Splatter painted a masterpiece, and George bounced higher than ever on the trampoline.

Nancy had to admit that the Flying Tremendoes were tremendous. Even Orson and the Chuckle Brigade made her laugh. As for Amy, she announced every act in style.

Nancy was a little sad that camp was over but glad that she'd solved her case. That night she wrote in her detective notebook:

Daddy was right. It's more important to tell the truth than do something that doesn't feel right later. I think Amy learned that this week.

I learned something, too. An elephant never forgets. And some of them make great detectives!

Case closed.

EASY TO READ—FUN TO SOLVE!

**Meet up with suspense and mystery
in The Hardy Boys® are:**

THE CLUES™ BROTHERS

Available from Minstrel® Books
Published by Pocket Books

Sabrina
The Teenage Witch®

Salem's Tails®

What's it like to be a powerful warlock,
sentenced to one hundred years in a
cat's body for trying to take over the world?
Ask Salem.

**Read all about Salem's magical
adventures in this series based on the hit
ABC-TV show!**

A MINSTREL® BOOK
Published by Pocket Books

2007-12